W9-BPM-436

Published in Canada and the USA in 2021 by Groundwood Books

The author acknowledges Mathieson Smith for his feedback on animal behavior and geographic range. Miigwetch, Mat.

Groundwood Books / House of Anansi Press
groundwoodbooks.com

Groundwood Books respectfully acknowledges that the land on which we operate is the Traditional Territory of many Nations, including the Anishinabeg, the Wendat and the Haudenosaunee. It is also the Treaty Lands of the Mississaugas of the Credit.

We gratefully acknowledge for their financial support of our publishing program the Canada Council for the Arts, the Ontario Arts Council and the Government of Canada.

With the participation of the Government of Canada
Avec la participation du gouvernement du Canada | Canada

Library and Archives Canada Cataloguing in Publication
Title: Mii maanda ezhi-gkendmaanh : niibing, dgwaagig, bboong, mnookmig dbaadjigaade maanpii mzin'igning / gaa-zhibii'ang Brittany Luby ; meznibii'ged Joshua Mangeshig Pawis-Steckley ; yaan'kinootngig Alvin Ted Corbiere miinwaa Alan Corbiere = This is how I know : a book about the seasons / written by Brittany Luby ; pictures by Joshua Mangeshig Pawis-Steckley ; translated by Alvin Ted Corbiere and Alan Corbiere.
Other titles: This is how I know
Names: Luby, Brittany, author. | Pawis-Steckley, Joshua Mangeshig, illustrator. | Corbiere, Alvin Ted, translator. | Corbiere, Alan Ojiig, translator. | container of (work): Luby, Brittany. This is how I know. | container of (expression): Luby, Brittany. This is how I know. Ojibwa.
Description: Text in Anishinaabemowin and English.
Identifiers: Canadiana (print) 20200282980 | Canadiana (ebook) 20200282999 | ISBN 9781773063263 (hardcover) | ISBN 9781773063270 (EPUB) | ISBN 9781773063287 (Kindle)
Classification: LCC PS8623.U217 M55 2021 | DDC jC813/.6—dc23

The illustrations were created digitally.
Anishinaabemowin translation edited by Mary Ann Corbiere
Design by Michael Solomon
Printed and bound in Malaysia

Kina ndawendaagnidog, giinwaa maanda
— BL

To all my relations
— BL

Nookmis, Audrey,
nshimsag, Blossom &
Biidaasmoseh,
Wasauksing First Nation gewe,
giinwaa maanda
— JMP-S

To my Nokomis, Audrey,
my nieces, Blossom &
Biidaasmoseh,
and the community of Wasauksing
First Nation
— JMP-S

Mii maanda ezhi-gkendmaanh
Niibing, dgwaagig, bboong, mnookmig dbaadjigaade maanpii mzin'igning

This Is How I Know
A Book about the Seasons

Gaa-zhibii'ang Written by Brittany Luby

Meznibii'ged Pictures by Joshua Mangeshig Pawis-Steckley

Yaan'kinootngig Translated by Alvin Ted Corbiere miinwa and Alan Corbiere

Groundwood Books
House of Anansi Press
Toronto / Berkeley

Aaniish ezhi-gkendmaanh niibing?

How do I know summer is here?

Pii dooskaabid Maang
wii-noondaagzid zaag'igning,
zhyaawshkozid Nimkii-dikman gewe gaazad
megwe-wiigwaas-niibiishing.

When Loon opens her red eyes
to call across the water,
and green Luna Moth hides
among birch leaves.

Pii Aamoo bbaa-maandoonmaang
zhaashi-jiibik, miinwaa
maamnanaabmangid Gaakaapshiinh
nbaad mtigoong.

When yellow Bumblebee collects purple
fireweed with me,
and we spy brown Screech Owl
asleep in the tree.

Pii miinan gaa-giizhiwaabidegin mgising
gzhaawngideg gewe negwiki.

When blueberries drop readily,
and the sand is hot enough to sting.

Pii mnidoonsag mookbizwaad megwemtigoonski zaawaabminaagog gewe ni-bngishmod giizis.

When insects billow black from the trees, and the sun slips into an orange dream.

Mii maanda ezhi-gkendmaanh niibing.

This is how I know summer.

Aaniish ezhi-gkendmaanh dgwaagig?

How do I know fall is here?

Pii pakweyaakshkoon zhoobaagshkaag,
miinwaa Memskon'gwiigaans ni-gziked.

When brown cattails swell and bend,
and Red-winged Blackbird takes his leave.

Pii Ninshib mwaad mndaamnan,
Mkwa gewe en’goonsan gdamwaad
en’googmig mkang.

When Mallard feasts on yellow corn,
and Black Bear licks the ant pile clean.

Pii zyaawaagin zhashkwedoonyin bebezhig bi-dpakiig, bbaa-bkibdooying dash megwaakwaa.

When orange mushrooms emerge one by one, and we collect them from the forest green.

Pii noondaash mnik aan'kwadoon zhi'oomgag,
ni-zhaawshkwaabminaagog gewe eshkam giizhig.

When white clouds form in fewer numbers,
and the sky seems bluer than it was before.

Mii maanda ezhi-gkendmaanh dgwaagig.

This is how I know fall.

Aaniish ezhi-gkendmaanh bboong?

How do I know winter is here?

Pii baabii’ag giizis wii-bi-gzhiiwaasged, gnawaabmagwaa gewe Waawaashkeshwag bnagaakmaawaad giizhkan.

When I wait for the sun’s bright light and watch brown Deer strip cedar.

Pii wiikshimag Gwiingwiish,
too-wheedle too-wheedle,
Baapaase gewe miin'kaanensan tamwag.

When I whistle to Blue Jay,
too-wheedle too-wheedle,
and lay seeds for red-capped Woodpecker.

Pii Waagosh bi-ndadmaaged ndashkwaandeming,
Waawaabgonoojiins gewe biindged giimooj
bbaa-nda-giizhooshing.

When orange Fox begs at my door,
and gray Mouse sneaks inside for warmth.

digen

Pii maamji-shpiming goojing dbik-giizis,
waasnoodeg gewe niibaadbik.

When the white moon sits highest in the sky,
and green light dances through the night.

Mii maanda ezhi-gkendmaanh bboong.

This is how I know winter.

Aaniish ezhi-gkendmaanh mnookmig?

How do I know spring is here?

Pii mkom ni-n'gizod,
zhaawshkobgoon gewe bi-dpakiig gooning.

When black ice softens,
and green shoots peek through white snow.

Pii Gyaashk bskaabiid wii-bi-saswin'ked,
bdagshkang dash zhiwi doo-saswining.

When yellow-billed Seagull comes home to roost,
and keeps her spotted eggs warm in the nest.

Pii Pichi boonang, nimoonsag gewe bbaa-dodminwaad miinwaa noonwaad.

When red-breasted Robin lays her blue eggs, and pink-bellied puppies tumble and suckle.

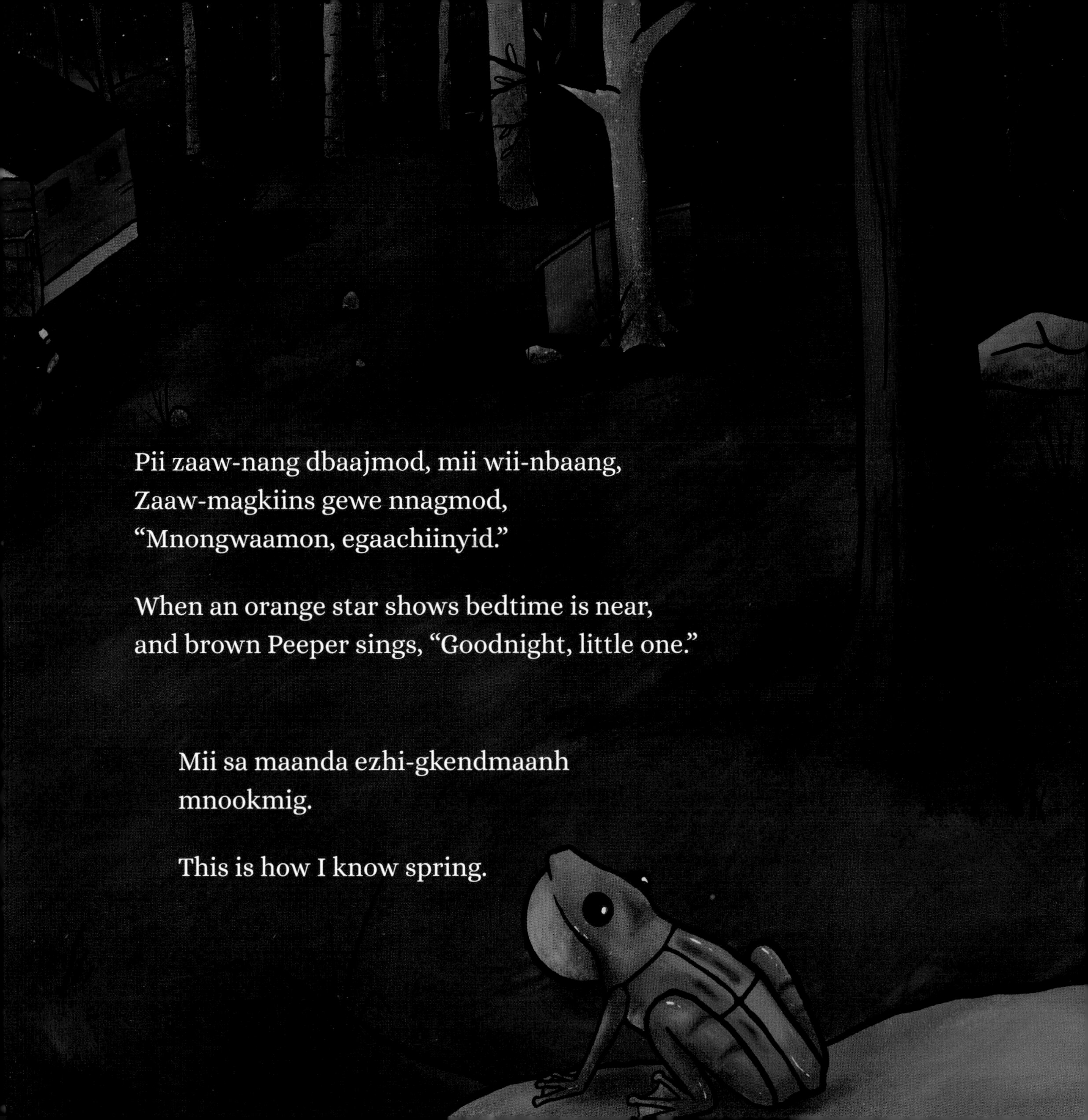

Pii zaaw-nang dbaajmod, mii wii-nbaang,
Zaaw-magkiins gewe nnagmod,
“Mnongwaamon, egaachiinyid.”

When an orange star shows bedtime is near,
and brown Peeper sings, “Goodnight, little one.”

Mii sa maanda ezhi-gkendmaanh
mnookmig.

This is how I know spring.